Kaimana didn't like being small. At school
he was always picked last on the playground,
and at home his older brothers never wanted
him around. If only he were bigger and stronger,
he would be at the top of everyone's list.

After school, Kaimana ran to Paki Park
and pulled himself onto the monkey bars.
Hooking his knees over the bar, he swung
back and forth, stretching his body with
all his might.

3

Upside down, Kaimana reached for the ground.
He twisted and twirled, swiveled and swirled
his body.

"What're you doing?" asked Cole, one of the
most popular boys in school.
"I'm stretching my body so I can get bigger,"
Kaimana said. Cole toppled over in giggles.
"That'll never work," said Emma, one of the
smartest girls in school.
"You're just a silly little kindergartener."

"Yes it will," shouted Kaimana, jumping off the bar.
"And I'm NOT in kindergarten! I'm in second grade!"
"It doesn't matter how old you are. You're just
a little baby," Cole said.

Kaimana went home angry. "I'm not a little baby," he frowned.
"What was that dear?" asked his mom. The savory smell of beef
stew drifted out of the kitchen.

"When am I going to get bigger?" asked Kaimana.
"You'll grow up soon enough. But, I've heard if you
eat all your vegetables, it'll help you to grow big
and strong," she replied.

That night, Kaimana ate all the carrots, celery and potatoes in his beef stew. For the rest of the week, he ate ALL the vegetables in every meal. On Saturday, he measured himself, but instead of getting bigger and stronger, Kaimana hadn't grown an inch!

"This isn't working!" Kaimana groaned. "I'll never be big and strong."

"Forget about being big and strong, Kaimana. Why don't you just go bodyboarding with your brothers?" said his dad. "Have some fun."

"Aw man, do we have to take him?"
whined Palani.
"Why not?" said Analu. "I took you, didn't I?"

7

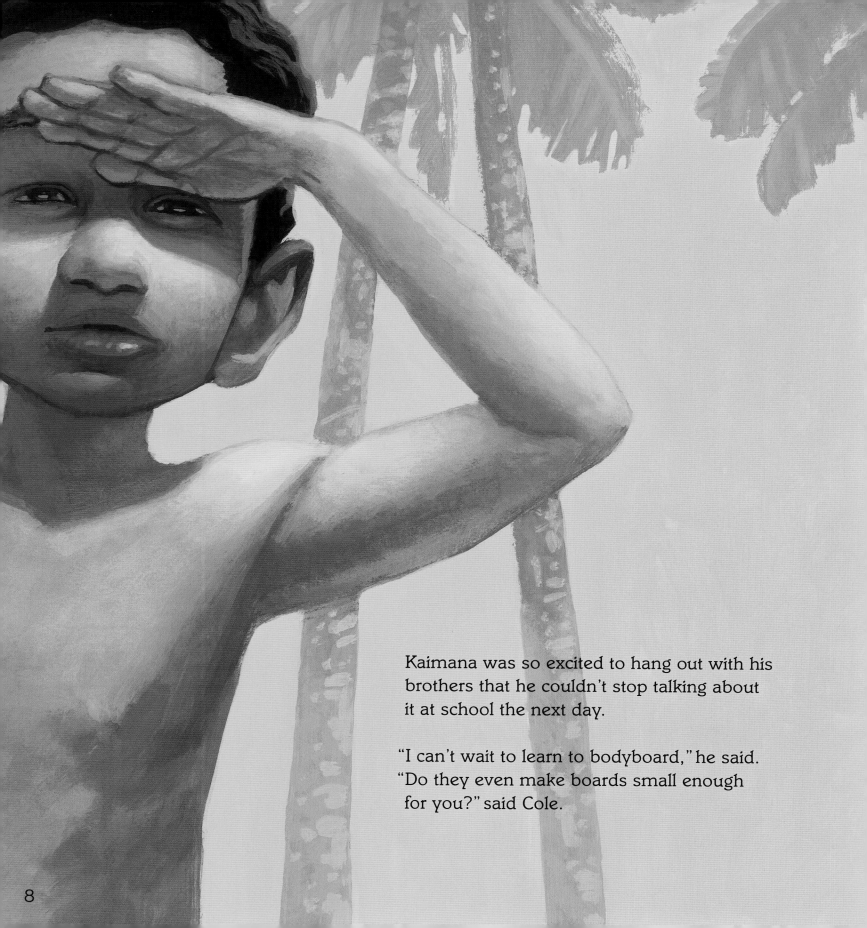

Kaimana was so excited to hang out with his brothers that he couldn't stop talking about it at school the next day.

"I can't wait to learn to bodyboard," he said. "Do they even make boards small enough for you?" said Cole.

After school, the brothers grabbed their boards and fins and walked to Kuhio Beach. Although Kaimana had grown up near the ocean, the big waves scared him and he usually stayed close to shore. *Today is going to be different,* he thought as they paddled out.

When the boys approached the breakwater, Kaimana began to get nervous. What if the other bodyboarders didn't let him into the lineup? Worse, what if they did and he couldn't even catch a wave?

"Good thing the waves are small today," said Analu.
"Yeah, good thing," Kaimana said, clenching his board.

They floated along as the older boys taught Kaimana how to read the waves and steer the board. Finally, Kaimana was ready to ride his first wave.

"When I say go, paddle as hard as you can," said Analu.
"Ready . . . Set . . . Go!"

Kaimana paddled and kicked furiously, splashing water everywhere, but the wave came and went without him. He tried again and again but never seemed to time it right.

After many false starts, a wave
finally picked him up and his board
shot down the tiny swell like a runaway
rollercoaster. The ride lasted only seconds
but to Kaimana, time stood still. He heard his
brothers cheering behind him.

Kaimana and his brothers went bodyboarding whenever there was a south swell. Soon he was making up his own tricks.
In the water, Kaimana forgot that he wasn't really big or strong. He didn't worry about the kids at school. He just had fun splashing in the ocean with his board.

Taking a shortcut through Kapiolani Park
one day, Kaimana and his brothers ran into
Cole and Emma.

"Where are you going with that board, Kaimana?"
asked Cole.
"We're going bodyboarding," Kaimana said.
"No way," said Emma. "You're way too little."
"I am not!" yelled Kaimana.
"Oh yeah? Well, prove it then," Cole said.
"Let's have a contest on Saturday to see just
how big and strong you are."

On Saturday, Kaimana was nervous. What if he wasn't good
after all? As he was leaving the house, Analu and Palani met
him outside.

"We have a surprise for you," Palani said.
"What is it?"
"I finished it in shop class yesterday,"
said Analu. He and Palani moved
aside to reveal a wooden paipo
board with a fiberglass finish
that glistened in the sunlight.

"Is this mine?" asked Kaimana.
"Sure is," said Palani.
"It's for your big day."

Palani and Analu walked Kaimana to the beach. When they got there, they saw a small crowd already gathered.

18

"It's about time," Emma said, putting on her flippers.
"We didn't think you'd show."
"What's that thing?" asked Cole.
"Does it even float?"
"Forget about them," Analu said.
"Just watch the sets and pick your wave."

Kaimana grabbed his gear and paddled out after
Cole and Emma.

19

The trio watched the swells rise and fall. Emma rushed the first wave in the set. She shot down the face, riding inside the barrel as the frothy water arced overhead. As the tube collapsed, Emma sped out the end.

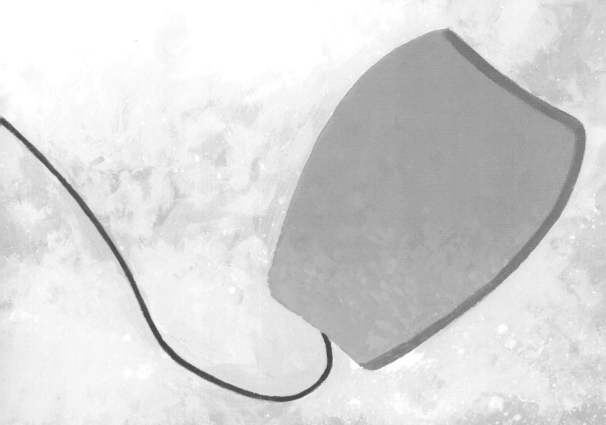

Off in the distance, another wave approached. It grew bigger and stronger as it came closer. Kaimana paddled as hard as he could. Out of the corner of his eye, he saw Cole paddling too.

"Coming through," shouted Cole, and he glided underneath Kaimana. Kaimana pulled back so he wouldn't hit Cole and let his perfect wave pass him by. Cole cut back and forth across the wave and spun 360 degrees.

"Whoo hoo!" called Cole. He tried for another 360, but the powerful wave broke sharply and crashed down on him. The rolling wave sucked him underwater, ripping his board off its leash. After a few seconds, Cole came up gasping for air.

Another wave was rolling in. This was Kaimana's chance to show everyone what he could do. He turned and pumped his arms and legs. His paipo board hung on the crest of the wave for a second before Kaimana angled the nose and dropped in. Perfect!

As he picked up speed, Kaimana glanced over and saw Cole splashing and sputtering, his head barely above water. Kaimana leaned sideways into a tight circle, letting the wave go by. He paddled over to Cole.

Out of breath, Cole reached up and
clutched Kaimana's outstretched hand.
"Are you okay?" asked Kaimana.
"Yeah, thanks," Cole said.

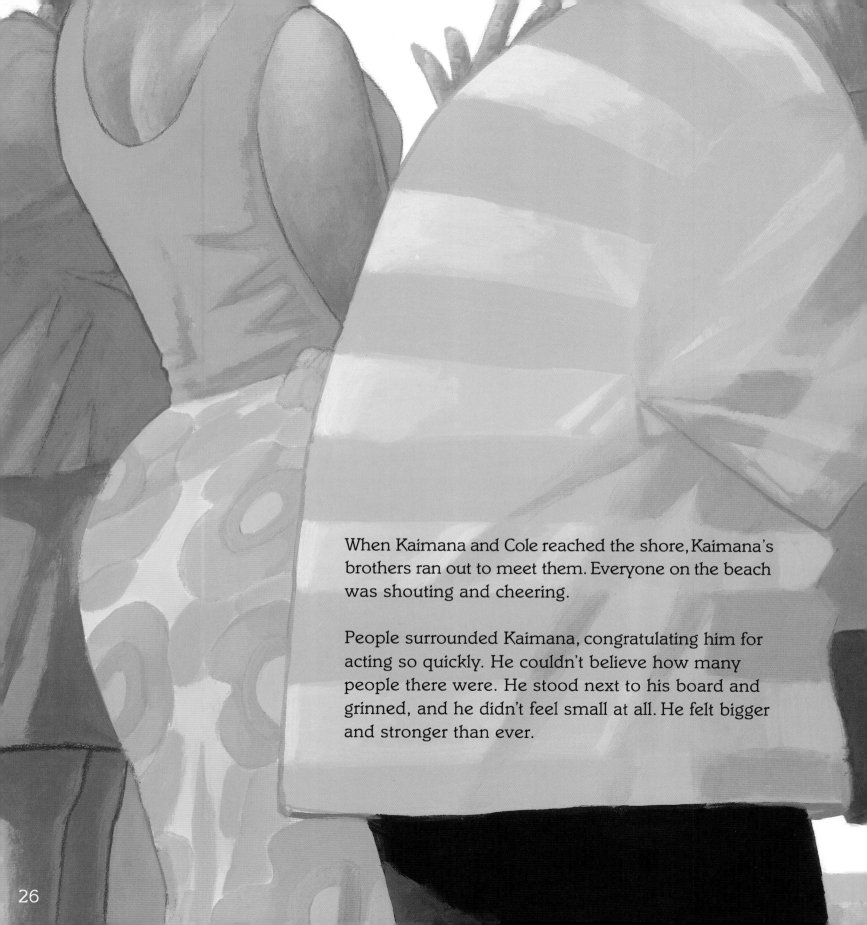

When Kaimana and Cole reached the shore, Kaimana's brothers ran out to meet them. Everyone on the beach was shouting and cheering.

People surrounded Kaimana, congratulating him for acting so quickly. He couldn't believe how many people there were. He stood next to his board and grinned, and he didn't feel small at all. He felt bigger and stronger than ever.